TOMMY   SIMON   CRISTIANO   STEVE   BERNARDO   YARA   IGOR

HONEY   MARIA   RUSSO   LUCAS   BOO   OFFICER AMARAL   CHICO

CARLA   BOB   JORGE   ISIDORO   SALGADO   LOUIS BUNNY   MR. ALBINO   NUNO

JOHN   NELO   DAVID   MR. SANTOS SOUSA

THIS EDITION FIRST PUBLISHED IN 2016 BY
GECKO PRESS
PO BOX 9335 MARION SQUARE
WELLINGTON 6141, NEW ZEALAND
INFO@GECKOPRESS.COM
REPRINTED 2017
TEXT © ISABEL MINHÓS MARTINS
ILLUSTRATIONS © BERNARDO P. CARVALHO
ENGLISH LANGUAGE EDITION © GECKOPRESS LTD 2016
TRANSLATION © DANIEL HAHN
THIS EDITION IS PUBLISHED UNDER
LICENCE FROM EDITORA
PLANETA TANGERINA
PORTUGAL

DISTRIBUTED IN THE UNITED STATES AND CANADA
BY LERNER PUBLISHING GROUP
WWW.LERNERBOOKS.COM
DISTRIBUTED IN THE UNITED KINGDOM
BY BOUNCE SALES AND MARKETING
WWW.BOUNCEMARKETING.CO.UK
DISTRIBUTED IN AUSTRALIA
BY SCHOLASTIC AUSTRALIA,
WWW.SCHOLASTIC.COM.AU
DISTRIBUTED IN NEW ZEALAND
BY UPSTART DISTRIBUTION
WWW.UPSTARTPRESS.CO.NZ
EDITED BY PENELOPE TODD
TYPE SETTING BY VIDA & LUKE KELLY, NEW ZEALAND
PRINTED IN CHINA BY
EVERBEST PRINTING CO. LTD
AN ACCREDITED ISO 14001 & FSC
CERTIFIED PRINTER
WWW.GECKOPRESS.COM

FUNDING ASSISTANCE FROM THE
DIREÇÃO-GERAL DO LIVRO
DOS ARQUIVOS E DAS BIBLITECAS

DG
LB
DIRECÇÃO-GERAL
DO LIVRO E DAS
BIBLIOTECAS

GECKO PRESS

DON'T CROSS THE LINE!

THIS IS HOW IT'S GOING TO BE. GIVE THE ORDERS AROUND HERE!

ISABEL MINHÓ MARTINS · BERNARDO P. CARVALHO
TRANSLATED BY DANIEL HAHN

SNiFF, SNiFF...

STOP!

I'M VERY SORRY, BUT NO ONE'S ALLOWED ONTO THE RIGHT-HAND PAGE.

BUT WHY?
IS THERE SOME TERRIBLE DANGER?
ARE WE BEING INVADED?
IS IT A DEMONSTRATION?

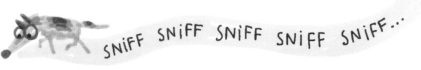

SNIFF SNIFF SNIFF SNIFF SNIFF...

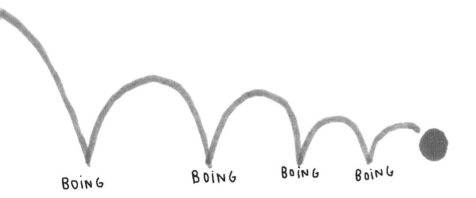

BOING BOING BOING BOING

THESE PEOPLE ARE SO CHILDISH!
LOOK AT THE STATE OF THESE PAGES! IT'S OUTRAGEOUS...

ME?

MARCO   SILVA   COSTA   RAFAEL   MADALENA   THE GUARD   GRUNF   LAETITIA

VIVI   ANA K.   HENRY   CAROL   MARCELINO   MR. SANTINO   ISABEL   BABO

JACK   VICTOR   NEIGHING-ROCKET   5   4   3   2   1   MOTHER

GENERAL ALCAZAR   MIRO   EDMUND   CHRIS   SAMUEL   PAT   PAULINA